■ この絵本の楽しみかた

● 日本文と英文のいずれでも物語を楽しめます。

● 英文は和文に基づいて詩のように書かれています。巻末Notes
　を参考にして素晴らしい英詩文を楽しんでください。

● この「日本昔ばなし」の絵はかっての人気絵本「講談社の絵本」
　全203巻の中から厳選されたものです。

■ **About this book**

● The story is bilingual, written in both English and Japanese.

● The English is not a direct translation of the Japanese, but
　rather a retelling of the same story in verse form. Enjoy
　the English on its own, using the helpful Notes at the back.

● The illustrations are selected from volume 203 of the
　Kodansha no ehon (Kodansha Picture Books) series.

Published by Kodansha USA, Inc.
451 Park Avenue South, New York, NY 10016

Distributed in the United Kingdom and
continental Europe by Kodansha Europe Ltd.

Copyright © 1993, 2013 by Kodansha USA, Inc.
All rights reserved.
ISBN: 978-11-56836-528-2
LCC 93-18501

First edition published in Japan in 1993 by Kodansha International
First small-format edition 1996 by Kodansha International
First US edition 2013 by Kodansha USA

Printed in Seoul, Korea, by Samhwa Printing Co, Ltd.,
arranged through Dai Nippon Printing Co., Ltd.
1st Printing, February 2013

www.kodanshausa.com

日本昔ばなし

ももたろう

THE ADVENTURE OF MOMOTARO, THE PEACH BOY

え●さいとう いおえ

Illustrations by **Ioe Saito**
Retold by **Ralph F. McCarthy**

KODANSHA USA

One day a long, long time ago
　　(*How* long? Nobody knows),
A woman we'll call Grandmama
　　was washing out her clothes.
The biggest peach you've ever seen
　　(I mean, a *real* big peach)
Came bobbing down the middle of
　　the river, out of reach.

"The water's bitter there!" she sang.
　　"It's made of fishes' tears!
The water's sweeter over here!"
　　Now, peaches have no ears . . .

むかしむかしの　おはなしです。
おばあさんが　かわで
せんたくを　して　いると,
おおきな　ももが
ながれて　きました。
どんぶらこ　どんぶらこ

4

But this one seemed
to understand
and washed up
at her feet.
She hauled it out
and took it home
for Grandpapa to eat.

おばあさんは
ももを　ひろいあげると、
いそいで　いえに
かえりました。

「これは　りっぱな　ももだ。」
おじいさんは　おおよろこびです。
そして　ほうちょうで
きろうと　すると，
ももは　ふたつに　われて，
あかちゃんが　でて　きました。

When he came home for lunch that day
    (he'd been out chopping wood),
Old Grandpapa said: "What a peach!
    Oh! Doesn't it look good!"
He got a knife to cut it, but,
    to his surprise and joy,
It broke in half, and—look at that!—
    out popped a baby boy!

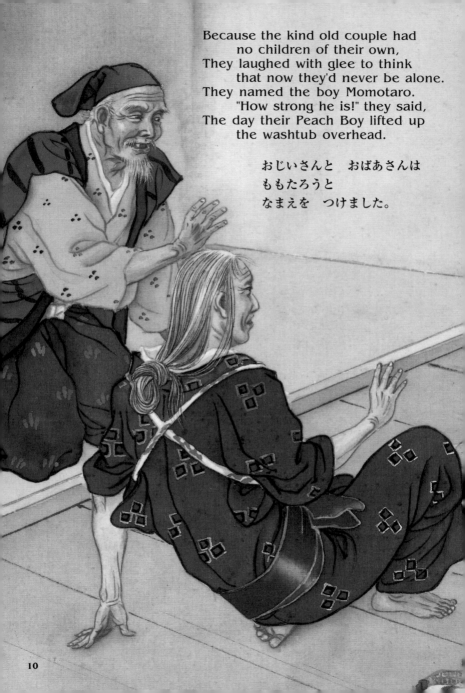

Because the kind old couple had
        no children of their own,
They laughed with glee to think
        that now they'd never be alone.
They named the boy Momotaro.
        "How strong he is!" they said,
The day their Peach Boy lifted up
        the washtub overhead.

おじいさんと　おばあさんは
ももたろうと
なまえを　つけました。

ももたろうは　すくすくと
おおきく　なりました。
こころの　やさしい
ちからもちに　そだちました。

As years went by, Momotaro
    grew stronger every day.
No sumo wrestler in the land
    could beat him, so they say.
What's more, he had a gentle heart
    (which no good boy should lack).
When Grandpapa was tired and sore,
    he'd rub his aching back.

ある　ひの　ことです。
ももたろうは　おじいさんと　おばあさんに
おにがしまに　おにたいじに　いく　ことを
はなしました。

Now, in those days, it seems,
　　　ferocious demons roamed the land,
Tormenting all the people;
　　　*some*one had to take a stand.
One day Momotaro said:
　　　"I must leave you for a while."
"But why, dear boy?"
　　　"To fight the demons."
"Where?"
　　　"On Demons Isle."

Momotaro asked Grandmama
  to make some millet cakes.
"Of course," she said. "You'll need
  your strength—that's what
    a battle takes."
She baked a batch
  of millet cakes—
    the best in all Japan—
And Grandpapa got out his sword
  to give the brave young man.

おばあさんは　きびだんごを　つくり，
おじいさんは　かたなを　だして
ももたろうに　もたせました。

ももたろうは
ふたりに　みおくられて,
おにたいじに
でかけました。

He took the sack of millet cakes
        and tied it to his waist,
And, since he was the strongest boy
        a foe had ever faced,
The banner that he carried read:
        "The Best in All Japan."
"Goodbye," he said. "I'll win this fight,
        if anybody can."

19

He marched across the mountains,
    where he met a spotted dog,
Who stopped him and engaged him
    in this little dialogue:
"Where will you go, Momotaro?"
    "To Demons Isle and back."
"What for?"
    "To conquer demons."
"Oh. And what's that in the sack?"
    "Some millet cakes."
"Please give me one. I'll keep you company."
    "All right, young dog. I like your style.
        Eat up, and follow me."

やまの　なかで　いぬに　あいました。
「ももたろうさん、　どこへ　いくのですか？」
「これから　おにたいじに　いくのだ。」
いぬは　きびだんごを　もらって、
おともを　する　ことに　しました。

They marched on through a forest,
    where a monkey said: "Hello!
Give me a cake, and I'll go with you,
    too, Momotaro!"
"Get lost!" the dog said, snarling.
    "No one wants an ape around."
The monkey turned bright red and said:
    "Shut up, you mangy hound!"
Momotaro said: "Stop that now!
    If we're to win this war,
We've got to work together.
    I'll have fighting here no more!"

つぎに　あったのは　さるでした。
さるも　きびだんごを　もらって，
おともを　する　ことに　しました。

The three were marching on
 across a wide, deserted plain,
And there they met a pheasant
 they could use in their campaign.
"Where to?" he asked Momotaro.
 "To Demons Isle and back."
"What for?"
 "To conquer demons."
"Oh. And what's that in the sack?"
 "Some millet cakes."
"Please give me one. I'll keep you company."
 "All right, young bird. I like your style.
 Eat up, and follow me."

ひろい　のはらで　きじに　あいました。
きじも　きびだんごを　もらって,
おにがしまに　いく　ことに　しました。

At last they reached the seashore,
    where they all got on a ship
To sail across the ocean
    on the last leg of their trip.
The monkey volunteered to steer,
    and pushed off from the shore.
"I'll paddle," said the dog,
    and put his paws upon the oar.
"I'll be the lookout," said the pheasant.
    "I can see a mile!
I'll raise a cry the moment I
    lay eyes on Demons Isle."

いよいよ　ふねに　のって，
おにがしまを　めざします。　いぬは
ろを　こぎ，　さるは　かじを　とり，
きじは　みはりに　たちました。

They sailed for many, many days
    (*How* many? I don't know),
 But then at last the pheasant
    shouted to Momotaro:
"I see it! There lies Demons Isle,
    a mile or two ahead!"
"Row faster, Dog, we're almost there!"
    the brave young captain said.

ももたろうは　とおくに
しまかげを　みつけました。
「おにがしまだぞー。
　しまは　ちかいぞー。」
ももたろうは　おおごえで
いいました。

On Demons Isle, the demons
    were sunbathing on the beach,
When one of them said: "Blow me down!
    I think I see a peach!
Hand me the spyglass, quick!
    Uh-oh! The peach is on a sail!
The sail is on a sailing ship
    as big as any whale!
I'm looking at a boy on board,
    and, boys, he's looking back!
We'd better tell the king—
    I think they're planning to attack!"

おにたちも　ふねを　みつけて、
おおさわぎに　なりました。
「へんな　ふねが
　こっちに　くるぞー。」

They ran into the castle, and
    they fell down on their knees
Before the Demon King, and cried:
    "Your Highness, if you please!
A boy approaches with a sword,
    a dog, an ape, a bird!
We think they're going to attack!"
    "What's that? Don't be absurd!"
The Demon King glared back at them
    with fearsome, bulging eyes.
"Just lock the gate. We'll sit and wait,
    and crush them all like flies."

「おやぶん、　たいへんです。
　こぞうが　いぬと　さると　きじを
　したがえて、　むかって　きます。」

32

The crew piled out
  upon the shore;
    the demons shook
      with fear.
The dog barked:
  "Open up! The Great
    Momotaro is here!"
The pheasant flew
  above the roof;
    the demons tried
      to hide;
The monkey climbed
  the gate and flung
    it open from
      inside.

「とびらを　あけろー。」
きじは　そらに　とび,
さるは　もんを
のりこえて,
　しろに　とびうつり,
　ももたろうと　いぬを
　しろの　なかに
　いれました。

The pheasant used
his beak to peck at
all the demons' eyes;
The monkey scratched
their faces; and the
dog chewed on
their thighs.
The King of Demons
raised his iron club
above his head.
"I'll pound your right
into the ground,
Momotaró!" he said.

いぬは　かみつき，　さるは　ひっかき，
きじは　めを　つっつきました。

37

おにの　おやぶんは
かなぼうを
ふりまわして，
ももたろうに
むかって　きます。
ももたろうは　みを
かわすと　おやぶんを
くみふせて，　うでを
ねじりあげました。

Our hero dodged about so fast, it made the king's head spin.
At last he fell (from dizziness) and landed on his chin.
Momotaro jumped on his back and gave his arm a twist.
"Surrender, fiend!" he cried. The king said:
　　　　　　　"Well, if you insist!"

おにの　おやぶんは
あやまりました。
「もう　にどと　わるい
　ことは　いたしません。
　どうぞ　ゆるして
　　ください。」

40

The Demon King knelt down
  before his youthful conqueror.
"I promise we'll be good!" he sobbed.
  "Oh, please believe me, sir!
And take this priceless treasure home—
  it's all we have to give—
A token of our gratitude
  (because you let us live)."

They put the treasure
   on the ship
      before they sailed away,
Then plowed off through
   the deep blue waves
      and snow-white
         ocean spray.

たからものを　つみこんだ　ふねは,
むらに　むかって　すすみます。

The demons lined up
on the shore
to bow and wave
goodbye.
"The strongest boy
beneath the sun!"
the king said
with a sigh.

43

They got back to the mainland
on a sunny summer day,
And put the treasure on a cart
and pushed it all the way.
To celebrate, they broke into
a funny little song:
"Heigh-ho, heigh-ho!"
they sang together
as they marched along.

はまに　つくと，
たからものは
むらに　はこばれました。

Old Grandmama and Grandpapa
          were waiting for their boy,
And when he rolled around the bend,
          they gave a shout of joy.
You don't see demons any longer,
          thanks to you-know-who:
The Peach Boy (and, of course,
          the pheasant, dog, and monkey, too).

おばあさんと　おじいさんは
みんなを　でむかえました。
ももたろうと　いぬと　さると　きじは
「ただいま，　かえりました。」　と，
げんきな　こえで　あいさつを　しました。

Notes   ももたろう ♦The Adventure of Momotaro, the Peach Boy♦

p.4　Came bobbing down ～　～をぷかぷか下ってきた　out of reach 手が届かない
　　　fishes' tears 魚の涙　have no ears 耳がない

p.7　washed up 流れ着いた　hauled it out それをひっぱり上げた

p.9　chopping wood 木を切りに　to his surprise and joy 驚き喜んだことには

p.10　with glee 大喜びで　lifted up 持ち上げた

p.13　As years went by 年ごとに　beat 負かす　What's more そのうえ
　　　which no good boy should lack それはいい子になくてはならないものです
　　　tired and sore 疲れて痛い　rub his aching back 痛む背中をさする

p.15　ferocious 恐ろしい　roamed うろついた　tormenting 苦しめて　take a stand 立ち上がる
　　　Demons Isle 鬼が島

p.16　millet cakes きびだんご　that's what a battle takes それが戦いに必要なもの

p.19　tied it to his waist それを腰に結んだ　the strongest boy a foe had ever faced 対決する
　　　敵には最強の男の子　if anybody can 必ず

p.20　engaged him in this little dialogue 次のように話しかけた　What for? なぜですか
　　　conquer 征服する　keep you company お供する

p.23　Get lost! あっちへ行け　snarling 歯をむきだして　mangy hound きたない犬
　　　We've got to ～ ～しなければならない　fighting here no more もうケンカはなし

p.25　deserted plain 荒野　pheasant キジ　campaign 征伐(せいばつ)

p.26　on the last leg of their trip 旅の最後の行程で　volunteered to steer かじ取りをかってでた
　　　paddle ろをこぐ　put his paws upon the oar オールに手をかけた　lookout 見張り
　　　the moment I lay eyes on ～ ～を見つけたらすぐに

p.30　were sunbathing ひなたぼっこをしていた　Blow me down! たいへんだぞ　as big as any
　　　whale 鯨ほど大きい　he's looking back! にらみかえしている　We'd better ～ ～したほうがいい

p.32　fell down on their knees ひざまずいた　Don't be absurd! ばかなことを言うな
　　　glared back at them にらみつけた　with fearsome, bulging eyes 大きな恐ろしい目で
　　　crush them all like flies 虫のように皆ひねりつぶす

p.35　piled out どっと降りた　flung it open from inside 中から門を開け放った

p.37　beak くちばし　peck at ～ ～をつつく　chewed on their thighs 太ももにかみついた
　　　iron club 鉄棒　pound your right into the ground やっつける

p.39　dodged about so fast とてもすばやく動き回ったので　it made the king's head spin そのた
　　　めに鬼の王の目はまわった　from dizziness くらくらして　landed on his chin ばったり倒れた
　　　gave his arm a twist 腕をねじ上げた

p.41　youthful conqueror 若い征服者　sobbed すすり泣いた　take this priceless treasure home
　　　この貴重な宝物を持って帰ってください　it's all we have to give これで全部です
　　　a token of our gratitude (because you let us live) (生かしてくれる)感謝のしるしです

p.42　plowed off 進んだ

p.47　rolled around the bend 曲がり角をまがった　thanks to you-know-who あなたがだれなの
　　　か知っているもののおかげで　　　　　　　　　　　　　　　　　　　　　　（佐藤公俊）